Nefertiti

Nefertiti

A NOVEL

Charles W Fowler

Commonwealth Books Inc.,

A Commonwealth Publications Hardback
NEFERTITI
This edition published 2023 by
Commonwealth Books
All rights reserved

Names: Fowler, W. Charles, author.

Library of Congress Control Number: 2022051526

ISBN: 978-1-892986-50-4 (hardback)
ISBN: 978-1-892986-51-1 (e-pub)

This work is a novel and any similarities to actual persons or events is purely coincidental.

First Commonwealth Books Hardback Edition February 2023.

PUBLISHED BY COMMONWEALTH BOOKS, INC.,
www.commnwealthbooks@aol.com
www.commonwealthbooksinc.com

Manufactured in the United States of America

Preface

Nefertiti was born in Egypt in 1370 BC. Her parents were assassinated when she was approximately five-years old. History recognized her when she married the Pharaoh at the age of fifteen. This is a fictional account of her missing ten years. All lies contained herein are the author's. This tale is told from the perspective of an observer or storyteller. I have no pertinent advanced degrees or actual experience that would make this story more believable, but I enjoyed writing it and I like Nefertiti. I hope the reader does, too.

One

On an early, soft, desert morning, a sentinel looking from his oasis toward the east saw a rosy, low haze. It wasn't a desert storm or dust devil. It was troops, attempting to abduct Nefertiti for ransom. There was nothing surprising about it. Pharaoh already took steps to defeat such an attempt.

The known world encompassed the shores of the Mediterranean Sea with a lesser well-known world and civilization far to the east. There weren't very many people in the world, and most knew each other individually or by family or tribe. No area was sufficiently populated to pose a creditable threat to his neighbors. The world was at peace, and trade abounded.

Those around the Mediterranean began trading with each other, using ships to cross the water. They had to deal with storms at sea and opportunists on land. Colonies were established along the long, desolate coastal regions of North Africa. Others were established along the southern Iberian coast and on Crete and Cyprus. Marbella was a favorite.

Some areas provided natural harbors and defenses. Others required artificial harbors and breakwaters. Ships became increasingly capable as thieves strived to steal their cargos whether on land or at sea.

During that early time in human history, the Phoenicians were the most-admirable seamen and merchants. They created defenses behind their towns toward the desert and sometimes around oases inland from the colonies. All countries were polytheistic, and their people felt free to kill, kidnap, rape, and steal from anyone whose religion differed, a belief that remained true for centuries afterward.

Two

Om, the sentinel, judged the approaching group was a small war party disguised as the crew of a reed barge hauling stone for future pyramids along the Nile. He reported the matter to Atli, the resident military commander and the surrogate and adoring father of the beautiful young girl who was the enemy's target. Atli sounded the alarm.

Armed men appeared, one from each family. There was no standing army. When the men were trained in military arts, the women worked the fields as well as their homes.

Atli trained his men well. He had been a mercenary until an emissary of the Pharaoh of Egypt approached him to secure his services for the protection of the daughter of a slain ambassador and his wife, making the girl an orphan. She was only four when she watched from under a vegetable wagon in Aktmim while her parents were assassinated.

Atli, ugly, monstrous in size, was covered with hair like a beast, yet the powerful soldier and tiny princess held each other's hands within half an hour, and the pact was sealed. Atli brought Om with him, a young soldier who studied Atli's technique to become the best soldier he could.

After two years with Atli, Om achieved near perfection, especially with the javelin. His javelin was tipped with a spearhead of volcanic glass, and it was rumored he never missed. It was also said that he never spoke to his target or used a battle cry, which made him more ominous. He was always within twenty meters of the little princess, even when she didn't know it. No one knew he was mute, but he understood even the slightest gesture from Atli and Nefertiti.

Om and Atli stepped forward with the princess between them, standing as tall as her six-years of age allowed. They trained well together. She placed her left hand on Atli's right forearm, leaving his spear arm free, because he was left-handed. Her right hand went to Om's left forearm, who was right-handed.

Behind Om stood a spear carrier with three javelins, while behind Atli stood a spear carrier with two heavy infantry spears. The last man in the formation was their runner, who would seize the princess and outrun all the other men to her barge on the coast if needed. Altogether, those were her Five Men.

Three

An came up early every morning from the savannah to the southwest to drink at the oasis. She saw the child playing with her best friend, To-To, with Om behind her with his javelin and felt content. She nursed her new cubs and played with them, licking them, as they swatted her under the chin, leaving behind a missing line of hair from cheek to cheek. Their claws weren't retractable yet.

Then came a morning when An saw rosy dust above the horizon. As a great cat, she was always curious. The approaching host saw the greeting committee and also noticed An on a hill behind her. They made an assumption and an error that the young lion was an adult, but An could snatch a 300-pound pig from his hole with one swipe of her clawed paw.

An was not a friend, and no one owned her. No one could own a cat. It was questionable whether a cat thought at all. It was said that a cat had no brain, just an ancient brain stem, and the only reason the cats hadn't gone extinct was due to their wonderful, retractable claws that all women envied.

The war party pressed on. If they couldn't kidnap Nefertiti, they could kill her and be richly rewarded in the next world.

The leader stopped forty feet from Nefertiti and smirked.

"She will be well cared for," he told Atli.

Atli shook his head once and hoisted his heavy infantry spear to his shoulder. At forty feet, he could drive the spear completely through the man's desert robe and body and hang his helmet on the spear point beyond.

Om remained ready but didn't move. A designated assassin sneaked into position behind the first line of troops. When he peeked at Nefertiti, she raised the index finger of her right hand to point at him. Om's spear went through the assassin's eye socket. There was only the flicker of an obsidian spear point, but Atli and An saw it with approval. Atli quickly speared the leader in the stomach, making the man scream and distracting the rest of the war party.

The Phoenician heavy infantry stood from their hiding places in the desert, and the raiders were routed. An no longer maintained her regal poise. Since a rout was a rout, she joined in, her cubs tumbling after her.

A woman saw the signal from Nefertiti to Om and the flash of obsidian. She was the wife of a warrior, and she ran back to tell the others, describing how the tiny princess, standing with her back straight and her hands resting on the men's forearms, ordered the death of her would-be assassin. The women's hearts nearly burst with pride and the knowledge that the girl wouldn't allow any foolish opportunist to kill one of their men. Nefertiti could fight, and she would kill if needed.

Four

Atli was no strategist, but he was a tactician without peer in the ancient world. He always had a plan ready in case of an attack. His plans varied depending on the size of the force, their experience, and their formation as they approached. He had several fall-back positions, and he made his men practice using them as regularly as for an initial engagement. There was no place in Atli's world for ad-hoc planning.

In Nefertiti's initial experience with combat, the opposing force was small, ill-trained, and approached between low hills in two files. It was as if a fly came to visit a spider in her web. The attackers saw only Nefertiti with five men to protect her. They didn't realize there were others behind both hills.

When their leader shrieked and died, Atli's men charged down the hills with heavy spears, and An joined the party. The few survivors told the story in such detail that it resulted in sculptures of Nefertiti doing battle with a sword while supported by great cats.

The truth was, she never engaged in combat or brandished a sword. All she asked of cats was that they smile.

Atli's men carried heavy Phoenician spears tipped with bronze. Their orders were never to throw such weapons. That reduced the soldiers from men to be reckoned with to unarmed men on a battlefield. Each soldier had a design etched into the shaft at the point of balance where he could feel it.

In the case of Atli and Om, the spear carriers dropped the next spear into the men's hands, as their arm rose to meet it just above the shoulder.

Most of Atli's weapons were hunting and farming implements of stone, the age that had only recently receded. Slingshots and stone axes were still issued and would be for many years. The tribulus was a small metal device of Roman design, made in a triangle such that it always had a point standing up. When a horse stepped on one in battle, it received a cruel wound to the soft part of its hoof and was immediately lame.

The Egyptian bow was a simple hunting bow from the past. Shooting such a weak weapon at an opposing soldier was tantamount to inviting him to kill a man. Long, recurved bows and crossbows were things of the future.

Atli taught the virtues of concealment, surprise, and speed. He made his soldiers take their ambush positions early so the dust of their movements had time to settle. Once in position, no man was allowed to move. They removed their helmets and looked over the dunes with their head flat to the ground, so only one eye showed. When the opposing foreman approached, the hidden men had to stay down behind the dune and listen only, to avoid being seen. Atli would face the enemy and give the signal.

The tactic was almost perfect, but on one occasion, Doobus shifted position and raised a small spiral of dust. Atli walked over to prod the man. When he walked away, the other soldiers taunted Doobus

"Do you itch? Do you have fleas? No? Lice? Have dung beetles found you pleasing? No? If Sheeba thinks you're pleasing to a dung beetle, she won't let you into the hut tonight."

They laughed.

A Hittite war chariot was captured. Since there was only one, and it was damaged, the men sent it to Atli for use as a swift courier between the oasis and the coastal town. Atli was glad to have it, but he had a warrior's heart and mind, so he studied it for that purpose.

He was impressed by how it could be used as cavalry. They would have to be accompanied by infantry on foot, which meant the soldiers had to run, and they would be exhausted when they fought, making them easy prey.

Atli had a longer deck built so a soldier could fight from aboard. Other suggestions were evident in Ramses' chariots when war with the Hittites came.

Atli gave the chariot and a young filly to Nefertiti for her amusement with the stern admonition that she not ride beyond the defenses of the oasis without Om and his choice of soldiers. Nefertiti and Moori, the filly, became inseparable. She groomed Moori, who nuzzled her in return.

A young man named Amun was chosen as Moori's stable boy. He saw to her needs and discussed them with Nefertiti as required.

Atli saw an opportunity. If Moori had a sturdy flatbed cart to pull, that would give her plenty of exercise and provide a means to carry larger loads from the coastal town. He promptly ordered the cart's construction.

Amun thanked all the gods and goddesses for permitting him to be appointed to his current position. He knew he could do Nefertiti great harm if he made her the subject of gossip. He heard many rumors from other nearby civilizations. Such rumors made great stories, but they could also result in serious loss to the royal personage, even death.

Amun taught Nefertiti everything he knew about horses, and she was an eager student. She saw him approach Moori gently, seeking her cooperation in whatever he wanted. He didn't try to master her, and they shared mutual affection. Amun breathed gently into her muzzle, and she answered the same way.

He taught Nefertiti about that by breathing on her neck. He explained how to care for the filly, showing her the proper direction to use a curry bone and how to use fingertips in tender places.

Every bit of this tutelage was done in public, with To-To and Om present. When Amun gently moved Nefertiti's hands along Moori's flank, she wondered if she was the one being caressed. She saw the care he took to protect her even when it was obvious to others. He was protecting her even from herself.

His hands stopped. Her knees felt weak, and she made an inane remark, but he knew. If either of them turned toward the other, they were lost. It wasn't supposed to happen. They looked into each other's eyes without smiling, showing dawning first love, urgency, and dread for the other's life.

A call came from the darkness. A nomad tribe needed the medicine woman. Amun ran to the nomads carrying a palm frond as a symbol of peace. The nomads struck their weapons into the sand for the same reason.

Morg was immediately behind Amun but kept his spear. Om stood behind him with his spear carrier next. Amun did quick triage, calling for To-To to send in the sick ones.

They were all children. Two injured men came, too. When they attacked the tribe, they were captured as slaves. A lone woman was another patient, because she had a breach birth.

Amun carried her at a run to the medical hut, hoping he was saving two people and not adding to her damage. The oasis children let the nomadic children in. The two men wouldn't be fed much by the tribe or the oasis people during the time it took them to become useful, so Nefertiti didn't expect to see them again.

She worked by touch with her small hands, following instructions from Ooze, their medicine woman, to save the breach baby. Ooze's strong, callused hands quickly had the tribe's children in much-better condition.

Moori, who understood what happened the previous night, was glad to escape without a hole rubbed into her flank.

Five

The oasis had one profound deficit—it couldn't feed all the denizens who relied upon it. Some food came overland from the coastal colony. Any human predator could see that weakness and use it. Atli intended to use it as bait in a trap.

The oasis provided great variety but not volume. It provided barley, wheat, rice, beans, lentils, onions, cucumbers, grapes, figs, dates, pomegranates, and peaches. There was sesame everywhere, because it grew in almost any environment. There was wine for the fortunate and beer for those who worked. There was even honey.

Honey was in short supply, because there was only one hive. When a man with more courage than sense went to steal from the hive, he was strictly told to leave one-quarter of the structure intact, so the bees could repair and add to it.

Nefertiti was addicted to sesame cookies made with honey. She knew honey would be hoarded for her if her desire was known, but she didn't want others to be deprived just because she liked something. There was no way to keep anything from the women's eagle eyes, though. Dozens of cookies arrived, and Nefertiti made sure every soldier had one with his midday bowl. She had two soldiers where only one had stood before.

She knew every mother saved a cookie for her own child. As an orphan, Nefertiti enjoyed the attention of all the women at the oasis. Also, she was a princess. The men's special duty was to protect her, and that conferred great prestige on the women in society. Woe betide any soldier who was dismissed by Atli.

He ordered that food storehouses be built to protect against future enemy action. They were quickly filled, but a great Saharan wind storm arrived, blew in through the doors, forcing the food out cracks and knotholes in the sides. For months, people joked that a soldier like Atli shouldn't thumb his nose at the gods of nature.

Still, he faced the problem of what to do if rations became short. The troops had to be fully fed. Combat in the ancient world was physical. He also had to consider pregnant women and nursing mothers.

Any future invasion had to come straight down the road from the coastal town in the north. Attempts from the east and west failed, and those from the south were defeated by the Sahara itself. When Atli escorted Nefertiti and To-To to the coastal town, he took troops with him to show them his plan.

They reached the secondary defense position when Moori gave an alarm by nickering and shivering. Intruders chose that day for a surprise attack. Atli didn't even need to bait his trap. He arranged his men for a surprise defense, with Nefertiti and Atli behind them. Amun was with the girls to see to Moori and provide a last-ditch defense.

Atli's men pounced with startling speed. His corps was among the nomads before they could react. Om had three dead at his feet, while To-To collected his javelins for reuse. Nefertiti crawled to Amun with two heavy infantry spears from the battle, so he would have weapons in the fight. The girls' actions weren't the result of training. They made every young soldier determined that he wouldn't be found wanting in the battle when stories were told around the campfires at night.

The intruders vanished, equally determined not to be part of the festivities when the fight was over.

Om had a slight injury to the top of his head. To-To sat beside him and crossed her legs, gesturing him to place his head in her lap so she could treat him with fingertips and salve.

Om stared up at her. She saw him stare at an opponent while measuring him for a coffin, but she doubted he was thinking of coffins when he looked at her.

There were two more serious wounds to other soldiers, which Nefertiti tended without a word.

Six

To-To was alone in the world, her parents having been assassinated, and her brothers and sisters all dying in childbirth or during early childhood. She became a street urchin and was picked up with the families going to garrison the oasis for protection and healing of Princess Nefertiti. A tomboy, she enjoyed the company of boys more than girls. She got into more trouble than the boys and fought dirtier. Word went out that no one wanted to get between To-To's weapon, whatever it was, and her target of the moment. She was wickedly adept with a slingshot, as many boys learned. Her favorite tactic was to ambush her victim and vanish.

She was taller and stronger than most girls her age, and they didn't like her. She carefully avoided conflict with girls, women, and animals, but she had no friends among them.

She couldn't compete with the boys in climbing trees, but she didn't know why. She suspected they were slightly stronger. She was lighter and more agile, so shinnying up the trees seemed better for her.

In her first try, she found that tactic didn't work, either. Her body became suffused with a delicious sensation, but it included weakness, forcing her to cling to the tree with her strongest grip to keep from falling. She didn't know why that happened and decided to consult Ooze.

When Nefertiti first appeared at the oasis, Om accompanied her. To-To thought wryly that the princess was showing royal prerogatives, but that thought was soon banished. Nefertiti was the nicest person To-To ever met. Her rank entitled her to have Om at her side, and he was devoted to her.

To-To took a fresh look at Om. It occurred to her that if any woman in the settlement became a widow, she would seek to become Om's best friend. Upon further thought, To-To decided she had to grow up soon. She needed to consult Ooze.

Seven

Ooze knew she was near death, but she still hadn't found a replacement for herself. She was the oasis community's medicine woman. She saw Nefertiti was often found early in the morning near the oasis, watching the wildlife from the smallest to the mightiest drink water and prepare for the day. Nefertiti paid attention to the plant life and seasonal changes that yielded seeds and nuts, as well as delicious vegetables that enhanced their diets.

The one person at the oasis who could learn quickly was the princess, but did the aging medicine woman dare approach her? Most of Ooze's duties included tending the injured, aged, or dying, and none of it was easy work.

Nefertiti probably wouldn't kill Ooze for asking, but Ooze didn't know what would happen from there.

When Ooze asked, Nefertiti accepted with delight. It was an easy next step. Nefertiti was always a visitor to a house where someone was ill. She began to learn about the medicinal value of the herbs and plants, fresh or dried. Ooze had a thousand years' worth of information in her brain, and there was very little time to pass it on.

Nefertiti, an avid, voracious student, worked Ooze as hard as Ooze worked her. She certainly extended the older woman's life and enriched her remaining days. Ooze was forty, the average lifespan of people in that time. They understood the world around them better than later generations, though they knew nothing of bacteria in food and water or infections in wounds. The water in the oasis was covered in scum from animal carcasses, urine, feces, and rotting vegetation. Sometimes children were sent to dive with goatskins to bring back clean water from below, but that was used for ceremonial purposes that had little to do with health.

Nefertiti was never able to add to Ooze's pharmacopoeia except for her discovery of a plant in the oasis that produced a hideously lethal sap if harvested and used wisely. Under normal circumstances, the sap was dangerous only to the plant's natural enemies. She confided her discovery only to Atli. If she told To-To, the girl would tell everyone.

To-To was very unlike Nefertiti. She was an airhead, a child of sunshine and laughter. However, if Nefertiti needed a helper with the sick and injured, she chose To-To.

To-To wasn't very interested in medicine, but she enjoyed her rare friendship with Nefertiti. She vowed never to disappoint the princess and soon learned the growing location of every available plant and herb. She also knew the locations of the storage areas and their contents. She had a solemn understanding with the other children that when she called, they had to come running, because Nefertiti needed them.

As people learned of Nefertiti's almost-magical abilities, she cared for an increasing number of people. Physicians of that time usually made people feel comfortable. It was people's belief in her that helped the most.

Soldiers were sometimes wounded in battle. It didn't matter to Ooze or Nefertiti who those men served. They would all be treated. Ooze noted from her long experience that wounds washed daily with clean water and freshly bandaged with clean linen seemed to have the best results. Nefertiti soon agreed with her. The recuperation times were long, sometimes as much as six months, but the two had a good success rate, and their reputation spread.

Sometimes, two combatants from opposite sides lay side-by-side and became lifelong friends during their recuperation. Others yearned for their enemy's blood as soon as they could move. To inspire those last to be at peace, Nefertiti produced a thin surgical blade, that the children kept razor sharp. She told the soldiers they would die from that blade if they misbehaved, but not from her hand but by To-To's. They understood and believed.

Everyone around the Mediterranean rim knew wounded soldiers were welcome at the oasis, but when they saw the medical hut, they had to lay down their weapons and come in alone. One didn't, so An ate him.

An wasn't impervious to injury. When injured, she became vulnerable to carnivores hunting in packs. When An didn't appear at the oasis for two days, Nefertiti asked Om to find her. He took an armed party and swept the desert southwest of the oasis, finding An had a good defensive position in a cave. She appeared to have a wounded left forepaw.

Nefertiti and Amun arrived with Moori and an armed party that evening. An sensed Nefertiti and smelled her medical kit. She understood what would happen and shivered. She saw Nefertiti treat many wounds, and she must not show her fear. Nefertiti wouldn't understand.

As Nefertiti approached the great cat, she knew she couldn't show any fear. An would sense it and not understand.

An plopped onto her side and turned up her wounded paw. Together, they got the job done.

Eight

Nefertiti slept on a bed of rushes in Atli's hut. Most nights, she crept into a ball under his left arm. She didn't think he knew or minded, but he always knew, and he cared.

On many early cool mornings, Nefertiti sat quietly on a sand dune looking at the dawn in the east. Some mornings, an asp rose behind her, and An ambled by to swat it into the reeds by the water where she lurked and waited for someone else.

Twice per year, the morning routine varied. Nefertiti bathed carefully in clean water and put on a soft white garment, embroidered at the neck with tiny red and green stones. She wore a small tiara, but there was no other adornment. Nefertiti was a beautiful child who required nothing more.

On those two special days, the princess inspected every hut in the village, as commanded by the Pharaoh. The women spent all the morning hours scrubbing and cleaning. The sand floors were lightly misted, then firmly patted with a piece of wood attached to a pole. When the women finished, no one was allowed inside until Nefertiti visited.

Each household prepared its favorite recipe, but the princess graciously declined them all. Later, those things would be offered to various gods, who accepted the offerings as a spiritual matter but otherwise left them untouched for the use of the family. One disapproving word from Nefertiti could shatter a woman's pride, but she was intelligent and sensitive, and she never said anything neg-ative. She was aware of her female neighbors lingering outside the windows of each hut, ready and willing to spread the good news.

There was never any record of Nefertiti raising her voice, grimacing, or being thoughtless or unkind. Even as a child, she was a sober person.

One time, Nefertiti and To-To went to see Ooze. They knew something about sex, childbirth, and menses, but they had incomplete information. Ooze was a medicine woman who had practiced for almost thirty-five years, and the girls asked serious questions, so the old woman told them what she knew, answering their questions.

Ooze assured them they could deceive men into believing in their virginity even after it had long since vanished. When they left, To-To was amused, and Nefertiti was determined to bring virginity to the table for her marriage. She was valuable and knew it.

Virgins and white lambs bore equal rank as sacrifices to the Egyptian gods. Egyptian men weren't fools and knew the gods were easy to please, so the flocks always bore that burden.

On their way back from visiting Ooze, Nefertiti and To-to noticed a small crowd of little girls around the medical hut. There was no taboo against peering inside, because the hut was open to the air and elevated to discourage asps and venomous centipedes.

Nine

Yet, it was considered impolite to look in upon the patients just out of curiosity. The girls approached quietly and saw that the pretty nurse. Viola, was attempting to shoo away a large green fly which was attempting a landing on the soldier's erection. She knew she was responsible for his condition and her futile ministrations were merely enlarging the problem. The soldier said. "Don't worry Viola. in just a minute I'll paste him on the ceiling." The little girls broke from their tip-toes and fled like a flock of little birds.

Early the next morning Atli sent for Viola. She shook in her sandals. She dressed in her medical hut gown. Surely Neferiti would intervene for her. As she walked she thought. Perhaps this was not about yesterday. She was small but very pretty. Boys took notice of her, teasing her and otherwise annoying her. but this was to get her attention or perhaps a smile. The girls were jealous and were perfectly happy to pass on tales about her which were untrue or only half true. at best. Anyhow. there was no avoiding Atli. He was the Pharaoh incarnate, with the power of life and death. If he had to send troops for her. there could be no simple solution. He would at least rumble in her ear leaving it charred. She went in.

Atli looked serious. He gestured for Viola to be seated on a stool and she sank upon it, grateful for its support. He wasted no time. He never did. Pharaoh wanted an agent in the camp of the Hittite king. This agent would be there for a limited time, ostensibly to conduct medical training. The Hittite king's request had been sent to the Pharaoh who approved it and sent it on to Atli. He, in turn spoke with Ooze. who recommended Nefertiti's fine young nurse, Viola. Would Viola accept this commission? Oh definitely! There had never been a female agent before! The concerns of only a few minutes ago were gone, as wisps of smoke on the air.

Viola was at the busiest time of her life for the next thirty days as Ooze gave her every wound to attend as they came in. It was well known that the Hittites were warlike: unnecessarily so. Then Moe arrived to transport her to Atlantis where she would board the Hittite royal barge for the final leg to the land of the Hittites. landing south of the small town of Troy. She was met by a delegation who expected a soldier/doctor. This was a young and very pretty girl. So pretty that the momentary speculation was that this was Nefertiti. With a moment to think they knew that this was Nefertiti's understudy, and therefore a true prize. Both their King's advisor and that of Pharaoh were standing there watching. This was no time to blunder. She was received with honors.

Viola worked hard from the start with a cloud of nurses around her. She explained what must be done in every case where it was possible to be effective. She explained the alternative treatments and why she made the choices that she did. When efforts would be wasted. she explained that also. They began to make a difference and this became known. Morale was affected in the army. Men did not have to believe that if they were hit they must die. or else rot to death within a few days. The soldier's women began to believe there was hope for their men. The nurses began to take real pride in what they were doing. They willingly worked the grim hours that Viola did. When she left the surgical tents she was accompanied by soldiers who considered it a privilege to protect her. When she emerged from her tent to go and see how things were going. she was immediately picked up and accompanied by new guards. Soon all the nurses were accompanied by guards. Eventually dogs were added. These quickly realized that they were not there to protect the guards. but to protect the patients and nurses.

Viola was conducting a class when she looked out over the heads of her students and saw a train of wagons approaching. She had been present long enough to know that this was wounded arriving from a battlefield. Even from a distance she could see that no initial care had been administered. The spears and arrows were lodged in the men's bodies and the bounce and sway of the wagons exacerbated the wounds. She directed the first wagon to the nearest surgical tent. Soldiers deposited the wounded man on the table unceremoniously. as was their custom. Men were expected to fight and if necessary die. Viola called her class to gather around. A quick analysis revealed a spear wound under the left collar bone. This vas a thrown spear at the end of its trajectory. There was hope. This same wound administered by a soldier with muscle behind it would already be fatal. Viola carefully dredged the area around the wound with vinegar then flushed with clean water. At this point she was ready to remove the spear.

She had seen the king enter with her excellent peripheral vision. but had not looked toward him or given any other notice of his presence. Viola continued to lecture as she worked. her eyes not upon them but upon the wound. Use only newly opened vinegar. Take what is left home for cooking or cleaning, but do not leave it in the surgical tent. Use only clean water. Here you are fortunate, for your city is built on a rock surface with water rising from far below.

Now. Soldier behind me. take the shaft of the spear in your hands. Hold it exactly as it entered the wound. Do not move it. When I signal. draw it out slowly along that same line. Start now. See, girls. A serrated edge. If we pulled it directly out it would have ripped more flesh. This way I can tease it out of the wound with a scalpel. As the tip emerges it is smaller than the width of the injury. Now. soldier. take the spear away. Viola pounced. working vigorously. Sweat poured from her brow. The soldier's hand came from behind with a cloth for the perspiration and to save her eyes from the stinging that could make them useless.

"Egyptian, you may have saved my son's life."

As they prepared to leave, the patient trembled and opened his mouth to cry out. Viola whipped the dagger from her girdle, flipped it in the air and dropped the wooden handle into his open mouth, whereupon he reflexively clenched his teeth upon it. She said. "If he cannot call out. he can walk out of here the same hero who was carried in." The King drew his dagger. leaned over and settled it into her empty scabbard. "When you have finished with your duties and have had a good rest, come talk to me about exervthing."

Thereafter, she was known as The Egyptian. even in Egypt.

Early the next morning she made her rounds and after checking that his son had slept well and was sporting fresh bandages. she sent a message to the King saying that she was available at his call. The messenger came back with an escort for her.

The king's residence was stark compared to other royal residences. Both of his wives had died in childbirth, of girls in each case. He lived vith his three sons and one surviving daughter, Elvira. None of them did anything to enliven the environment. He felt lonely in his own home.

The conversation began with the King's question about Viola's observation that there was no initial care. She explained that the wagon ride to treatment could be fatal to wounded men with arrows and spears still in them. It was as if an insane enemy with a mean streak was on the other end of the weapon. The King should send nurses with the wagons. Here the King interjected that he did not favor getting young girls killed. They were his most valuable resource. the infant mortality rate being what it was. A girl was worth her weight in Chamois skins, when the skins could be found. Viola brought him back to the mortality rate by asking him why his people's rate was better than that of most. The King pointed out that people living high in the mountains and on seacoasts not beset with gritty sandstorms enjoyed a similar reputation. He noted that the Hittites lived on bare rock. There were winds, but they were free of grit most of the year. There might be a correlation there. Pure water found in these places may have meaning as well. The King did not believe it could possibly be good for anyone to drink water that could be smelled.

The King and Viola continued their conversations on a regular basis each becoming more fond of the other. The subject matter of their talks was leaked to the rest of the population by the household servants. The hope was that the king would heed the Egyptian's advice and be persuaded by her philosophy. Everyone knew that all of that sound thought could not have been developed in that one small head so early in life. She vas the product of a culture at its height.

One day the King proposed they go for a ride to visit the small agricultural portion of the Kingdom. Viola protested that she had never ridden a horse. He guessed as much and produced a pair of war chariots. These were beautiful machines and were prepared carefully in advance for the enjoyment of The Egyptian. Her safety was assured by an escort of mounted cavalry. all proud to have been selected for this duty. The King mounted one of the chariots and Viola was directed to the other. She visited the mare first and greeted her as Nefertiti had taught her. She mounted the chariot and discovered that her driver was Elvira.

The king's three sons also took interest in Viola. but not in deep conversation. It did not hurt that she was a very pretty girl, soon to be a real beauty. Elvira sulked.

Evan, the son who survived under Viola's ministrations, was pleased that The Egyptian had Elvira sulking. He was also very pleased with her popularity with the people. Privately, he was grateful for her dagger handle in his mouth when it was needed. Life could go on.

The King walked with Viola in the fields of grain and the orchards and vineyards. There he told her how the Hittites had left the frozen north and had made it this far. Here they found high bare ground and good water. The fields of fire on all sides of their colony were excellent for defense and survival. That ended the good news. Food within their ovn lands was far from the center of their civilization. They had treaties with all of their neighbors which had worked well for all concerned for years. but treaties could be broken. They traded for grain with the Egyptians each year. but the Egyptians were overdue for a hoard of locusts. They were immobile. They could not go back to the frozen wastes of the North. The West offered no road to safety and self sufficiency since the Greeks were there and laid claim to every island in the Aegean Sea. They would cheerfully, temporarily cease killing each other to repel an invasion from the East. They had the navy for the job. too. They could not rationally move east since the hordes from there would then be within range and they typically killed every living thing before them. A move south would be against good neighbors. These people had ceased their own migrations at the shores of the Mediterranean sea where they built good lives and walled towns. The Hittites had simply began their own migration too late in the day.

No nearby civilization wanted their land for any reason, so no one else was going to relieve them of their problem. The King asked Viola to think about his dilemma and give him her thoughts when they had the chance to speak again.

The king asked what Viola thought of his agriculture. She replied that he had poor land, but could expect better crops from better tools. The farmers were using heavy bronze hoes and scythes which were crude and unsharpened. The King agreed. and asked what would improve matters. She explained. They were chipping at the bronze, They needed to hone it to get a long. keen edge.

Viola stopped the procession to demonstrate. She found a smooth, flat rock, sprinkled the finest sand she could find on it. then spat into the sand. She then rubbed a soldier's spear across the gritty surface until she had a new edge.

Elvira suggested that a better grinding paste could be made with more water than spit provided. She suggested that Viola could provide the greater amount here and now. Viola and the King smiled small. private smiles and the King shook his head slowly. Mount Elvira was ready to erupt. It was time for The Egyptian to go home.

Ten

Morg, the oldest warrior at the oasis and the first to follow Amun into the nomadic camp, was their local drunk. His long, heroic service earned him a place in the unit, but that came with a price. It was said he could drink a clay urn of beer in the evening without stopping to urinate and would pass out in the graveyard while conversing with the dead. Asps refused to attack him, fearing his blood would prove lethal. Poisonous scorpions snuggled against him at night for his body heat, but they didn't sting, because that heat was important. They relied on him to return to the same place to sleep every evening.

Little children usually avoided the graveyard at night, but with Morg's arrival, they avoided it even more.

Ooze had no fear of the dead, but she dreaded passing near Morg. His odor could wilt water lilies. He generated horrible gas that made men's eyes water and destroyed their depth perception. Carrion birds refused to fly over him.

It was well-known that Morg was interested in Ooze, but she had guile and enough speed to elude him.

When Nefertiti found out how old Morg was, she asked why he hadn't died yet. He replied that the various nice deities weren't ready for him yet, and the evil ones didn't want him to compete with them.

It was rumored that the gorgons were in awe of Morg, and Medusa would swear to it. According to his reputation, Morg never left an opponent alive after a battle. When he was asked about that, he modestly admitted it was true, because he didn't want a spear in his back from a wounded enemy. He returned later to eat their livers.

Enemy soldiers avoided Morg on the battlefield, not only because they feared him, but because they didn't want him to desecrate their bodies. Oasis men advised their women that if the camp was ambushed, they should stand behind Morg. They would be safe as long as he didn't turn around.

Atli summoned Morg to his hut and told him that he had just volunteered for a dangerous mission. He had to select six expendable volunteers and meet Moe, the ablest seaman on the Mediterranean, at the coastal town. Moe would take them to Malta, where they would seize little Ty from her abductors and bring her to the oasis. The girl had been traveling with her parents in Carthage when she was taken. A local witch pointed her out, hoping for a finder's fee.

The ransom message was pleasantly worded, citing the amount desired, either in gold or Roman coin. A prompt reply was recommended, because Ty had only olives to eat. If payment lagged, the captors would spit her on a spear and roast her.

The plan was simple. Moe would land his armed party on Malta's southwest coast in the abandoned village where the scruffy rascals held Ty. Morg was allowed to improvise as he saw fit.

Moe's party landed near midnight with the advice they should approach the village on the beach, because the inland route was rocky and noisy. They found all the captors asleep or passed out from drinking. Hearing restless sounds in one particular hut, they moved toward it.

From a rear window, Morg saw Ty standing on her bed, staring at him. He swept her up out of the window and hugged her.

"How'd you know we were here?" he whispered.

"You stinked."

They retraced their way to the ship, with Ty being carried by someone who had bathed that month. Moe brought his boat to shore, and by dawn, they were comfortably on their way to Carthage. Fishing smacks from Sicily converged on Malta from the north, their attention on a small fire on the river near the huts. Morg delayed pursuit by burning the captors' boats, and the fire produced another benefit. The would-be abductors would be frustrated to find Ty missing and would take slaves to make their lost day of fishing worthwhile.

All was right with the world. Moe would never be caught by fishing boats.

The party in Carthage lasted until morning, with the adventure being retold many times. The part where little Ty described how she knew she was being rescued brought more laughter the more often it was told, and Morg laughed louder than anyone. Praises were sung for Moe's successful plan, and he was honored with the singing of sea shanties about sailors conquering storms, gales, pirates, sirens, and witches.

The mention of witches sobered him enough to realize that the core problem hadn't been addressed yet. He went to find the witch who expected to profit at Ty's expense. As he sought her, more and more people offered to help him. He accumulated a great crowd that trailed behind him.

When he found her, he greeted her with a respectful bow, then he opened a hole in her throat with his spear point. All agreed that stripping a witch of her power of speech was an appropriate punishment that would serve to warn others.

Morg's reputation lasted a thousand years.

The trip to the oasis was an occasion for rejoicing, but Morg maintained a sharp lookout. The pursuers didn't have to stop at the water's edge.

When the little caravan came within view of the palm trees of home, Morg held Ty over his head so the sentinels in the treetops could report his success to those below.

They arrived to find a welcome party in full swing. People composed a song of joy, awaiting the details to flesh it out. Moe and his crew led the parade, with Morg and his raiders flanking little Ty on a war chariot to bear her to the fiesta. She was the honored centerpiece of the greatest celebration any of them saw. Egyptian music usually played on harps and woodwinds, with a religious, haunting sound. That day, the singing was lusty and soared into a paean of victory. Ty was a princess that day, and Nefertiti was proud of the people who gave the little girl a day to remember.

Atli summoned Morg, who hadn't started on his own beer or sought Ooze. Atli needed advice, not a volunteer.

The Pharaoh was told by his resident College of Surgeons that there was a substance called *natron* that had the consistency of fine powder and would absorb seven times its weight in water, which would greatly speed the process of mummification. It was already being used to mummify cats. Extremely rare, *natron* was found only in southern Africa. Could the oasis form a team to investigate that claim?

Morg admitted he knew of the substance, but it was a three-year round trip to secure it. They would meet fierce natives who loved fighting more than life. When preparing for combat, the natives chewed the leaves of a bush that prevented them from feeling any wounds or fatigue. There were as many of the natives as a blight of locusts. If they decided to come north along the Nile, they would destroy the Egyptian culture within a year.

Atli knew Morg wasn't exaggerating, so the Pharaoh stopped the project.

Atli summoned Morg, Om, and Moe and told them he needed advice on a few things. Such an admission of human fallibility stunned them into silence.

He recalled how Nefertiti recoiled from the assassination of her parents to the point that Pharaoh established the oasis as a base for a corps that would support her solitude and recovery. He arranged for the men to bring their families, so the oasis wouldn't be a barren military camp but a living village. Animals were allowed safe passage to and from the water, all in an attempt to aid Nefertiti.

It occurred to Atli there was little variation from day-to-day. No one wore different apparel, spoke another language, or showed a wide variety of goods to sell. Those were things a highly intelligent young princess needed to experience before moving to the royal court. She had to be exposed to as many cultures as possible. How could they do that?

Moe admitted he felt the same thing since he brought Ty back from Malta. "Nefertiti should sail with me for a few years. Then she would know the people of the world so well, she could guess their thoughts before they had them."

"That sounds good," Om said, "but I should go with her as her bodyguard. I've been with her for her entire life. We should appoint To-To as her lady in waiting to accompany her. It wouldn't be good for Nefertiti to spend all that time alone among sailors. Ooze would make a fine mature companion, but the oasis needs her. Since To-To is only a few years older than Nefertiti, they could have a fine adventure and train for the future."

"I recommend we send spies to all the expected ports of call to assure the princess' safety," Morg said.

"These things sound good," Atli said, "but we can't impose them on her. She must think of it herself."

"How will To-To deal with the idea of being a lady?" Morg asked.

They grinned at the idea. To-To's Egyptian name was that of an edible cracker, and she would never allow anyone to call her Lady Cracker. Lady To-To would have to serve.

Atli kept his final thought to himself. If he sent Morg, penned up on a small ship, the crew would likely mutiny and maroon him on a deserted island. Would anyone care? What about Ooze?

He changed his mind and continued the conference, asking that Doobus, Amun, and To-To to join them.

When they arrived, Atli said, "The oasis won't survive as an outpost more than ten years. Oases appear and disappear naturally all the time. By that time, Nefertiti will be on the Nile. We must focus on what the world will be like in ten years' time and help her plan for whatever she must face then."

The others agreed to think on it and meet again in thirty days.

To-To stayed behind to talk with Atli after the others left. "Why didn't you ask Nefertiti to participate in this discussion? Why did you summon me with Doobus and Amun? We're very junior here."

"Nefertiti will be queen someday. She must be free to reject any plan made without her personal involvement. Doobus isn't the most-glittering stone in a tiara, but when you consider future combat, he is the best field commander. Amun knows more about horses than any of us. You needed to know what we're planning and why, for the day when she asks you."

Regarding her thoughtfully, he decided to explain the rest of it. "Egypt has no standing army. The oasis provides a cadre for a splendid officer corps. Reservists can train under them."

The reservists would be equipped with a new bow based on the one the Hyksos used. It was a bow made of laminated strips of wood and leather, cemented together with glue made from fish products. It required eighteen months to cure, and production had to start soon if Egypt were to have the thousands of bows needed in a war. Chariots had to be redesigned with short beds for speed and agility to take advantage of the new bows.

They would also need a navy, with Moe as their admiral. The Phoenicians could recommend volunteers, and Moe even had some friends among the Vikings who would enjoy training them and leading them in battle as mercenaries. The Romans were improving their fleet daily. If Egypt didn't launch a fleet soon, Moe would have to lead the Roman fleet into Carthage harbor, where it would fall under the Carthaginian sword. The only other option was to have Moe lead the Romans out through the Pillars of Hercules, where the Atlantic would take care of them.

The current royal guards were so inexperienced, they were a danger to themselves and the present Pharaoh. If he was intent on having his son succeed him, he might be persuaded to delay stepping down from the throne until the new military was in place and well trained. If the new Pharaoh decided to banish the worship of all gods but one, not only would clerics be out of work, but thousands of stone masons would be at loose ends. Perhaps the Pharaoh could be persuaded to require his son to seat Nefertiti beside him on the throne.

To-To nodded. "We need a plan to transfer all human resources to the Nile with Nefertiti. She shouldn't be required to learn to live among strangers in her own country twice in her life. She should be sent to visit her only living relative, her sister, Mut. If the Pharaoh agrees to the plan, the people should be told about their future. That will stop any rumors and calm the insecure ones."

Atli nodded. "I'll send your suggestions to the Nile immediately."

To-To left, sobered by the meeting and by the Pharaoh who trusted Atli so much.

When the Pharaoh learned of the proposed plan, he sent a brief message: *Execute the plan*

Eleven

Moe, a Phoenician, had a reputation as a superb seaman and naval warrior. He was responsible for Nefertiti's safety at sea and from invasion by sea.

The commercial colonies around the rim of the Mediterranean were from many countries that were extended families or tribes. They moved around the shore without any limitation imposed by defined borders or the many languages and religions among them. Defined borders had to wait until the British arrived centuries later.

The languages were polyglot and well enough understood by businesses. The religions began with the sun, moon, and stars and moved on to whatever gave mankind hope. The people living along the Nile delta and the Nile south of Thebes were known as Egyptians. Slowly and peacefully—for the most part—they absorbed the smaller colonial peoples.

That didn't trouble Nefertiti, who thought there was strength in numbers. She felt Rome was getting too arrogant and perhaps too drunk on bad wine. There was little reason for it. Rome had little to be arrogant about, and the best wines were produced along the southern shores of the Mediterranean.

The ancient Egyptians didn't normally keep slaves. When prisoners were taken in combat, they were executed by the victorious commander unless he was inclined to be merciful, whereupon he had them castrated.

Uninvited immigrants weren't treated well, either. The colonies filled with workers from local countries and were supported from there. Immigrants from Africa below the Sahara were hunter-gatherers, who didn't work. Herding animals was still centuries in the future. Since there was nothing to hunt or gather in most of the Sahara, they sought handouts. They were often given only a cup of water and then sent south at spear point. Predictably, they protested that they were hungry and saw food was waiting in front of them. When they were told they had to exchange work for food, they were astonished. If they returned after being sent away, they would be killed and left for the carrion eaters.

The Romans, an increasing nuisance, assembled enough population to begin to assimilate the lesser cities of Italy. In the process, they created an excellent army for land battles. However, the army had to be transported in ships, which faced the tender mercies of sailors like Moe. The Romans used biremes, and, later, triremes, but the ships were never allowed to reach shore so the army could fight a land battle.

The ships were propelled by slaves using oars, with several men chained to one oar. When the Roman ships were caught by the faster, more-nimble trading vessels, men like Om killed the slaves with fire javelins. In the resulting chaos, they lost their steering oars and were defeated.

Whenever a Roman ship ran aground on rocks, the harpies of the shore were waiting. The colonists revered their courageous seamen, while the Romans, who no one revered, increased taxes on their own people to support an even bigger military to protect their status quo.

The Hittites were also becoming an annoyance, although there was no obvious reason why. Their statesmen concluded treaties with the nations near them, and in all cases, they kept the peace and advanced the prosperity of all parties, yet the Hittites weren't Semitic like their neighbors. They came from north of the Black Sea. They were warlike by nature.

They kept improving their plans to invade Egypt, even when they knew Egypt had no intention of attacking them. Some thought one of the Hittite kings had visions of military grandeur. Fortunately, he had a good statesman to advise him.

The statesman explained the pros and cons. The Hittites had no navy, while the Egyptians had the Phoenicians. They also had excellent sailors of their own with endless experience on the Red Sea, the Nile, and the Mediterranean.

The Egyptians also had the Sahara. Throughout history, no invading force ever returned home intact from attacking Egypt.

Then they had Nefertiti, who was so well-loved and admired in every country in the known world that the Hittites would quickly find every man's hand turned against them. Her name would resonate down the ages, while the king's name would be forgotten when his successor mounted the throne.

To his credit, the king heeded this advice.

Twelve

Moe decided a quick run to the Iberian Peninsula for a more-detailed study of the visiting Viking craft was worth his time. The Vikings were called Norse, Norsemen, or Northmen. The term Viking didn't come into vogue until the ninth century AD. Although Nefertiti lived from 1370 BC to 1330 BC, the Vikings were known to visit the Mediterranean.

When news of the planned trip reached Nefertiti and To-To, they went to Moe to request passage to Iberia and back. He tried to dissuade them, but they heard of cosmetics, perfume, and jewelry in Hispania that couldn't be found anywhere else in the known world.

That was true. Moe knew that caravans from the East went there, sometimes taking two years for the round trip.

Moe spoke to Atli, who asked a few wise questions. The answers showed that nothing the Romans had could ever catch Moe even in a gale, as long as he wasn't burdened by necessities for the coastal town or oasis.

Atli checked the inventory and saw that a cargo of grain could be forgotten for that trip, while a cargo of valuable but light items would assure Nefertiti's safety. He gave Moe his blessing. When Nefertiti learned of this, she hugged Atli so hard, he was almost knocked off his feet.

That was the first of only two emotional demonstrations of love history recorded about Nefertiti. The second was a bad sculpture of her kissing her husband, the Pharaoh.

Moe plotted a course that would taken him to a Spanish destination where he could grant Nefertiti's wish and also get a good look at the Viking ships. He had been there many times and knew many people who could help ensure Nefertiti's safety.

On the trip north, the girls were told to obey any order from a sailor of any rank and without question. That was a new thing for Nefertiti, but she accepted it. It wasn't new to To-To, though, and she felt rebellious despite knowing it was necessary to free at least one sailor from controlling them so he could manage his ship.

When the moon rose, Nefertiti encouraged To-To to join her in flipping the skirts of their one-piece garments to moon the Moon Goddess and see what would happen. They shrieked with happiness and admired the hiss of white water moving past the hull. Despite their sacrilege, nothing bad happened. Nefertiti, who didn't believe in any god or goddess, wasn't surprised. To her, the face of the Moon Goddess resembled a man, anyway.

In the morning, they mooned the Sun God, and again there was no repercussion. If there were any gods, they had to be sleeping or just didn't care.

Moe approached the coast with care. At the horizon, he lowered his sail, and all eyes studied the shore. When they were satisfied it was safe, they raised the sail to take the ship into the channel with her port side to the commercial dock.

Stevedores came up to relieve the ship of its cargo. Moe wanted to unload and reload quickly to avoid any Romans descending upon them when they couldn't get under sail quickly.

The stevedores knew that and weren't surprised when Moe waved his arm toward the town to request more help. People approached. When he saw three particular women among them, he ordered the work to begin.

Once the stevedores unloaded the ship, they lined up to be paid. Moe placed a Roman coin in each man's hand and also paid the three women who had lost their men in combat and had children to feed and clothe. It wasn't charity. The women worked alongside the men and earned their wage. They almost worshipped Moe for hiring them, and the merriest moments of their lives came when his ship hove into view.

Moe visited two Viking ships and crawled through them. Vikings arrived to chat, and two different cultures arrived at nearly identical solutions to nautical questions. Their talk lasted through the night.

The Northmen had only one suggestion for Moe. He should paint his ship as gray as the sea on an overcast day. If he had only one corsair, that would make his ship nearly invisible. The Vikings didn't do that, because they wanted to be seen and feared. The shock of their ships arriving off anyone's coast was worth an additional two dragon ships.

Moe offered a suggestion concerning naval tactics that the Vikings liked. The three agreed to bring naval architects when they returned in the spring, who could easily make alterations to similar ships. The raw materials in Iberia were superior to and more plentiful than those of the desert or the icy north.

Nefertiti and To-To had a wonderful time. To people who lived in a rural setting, visiting a town with businesses on every corner and bazaars in each square was exhilarating. Their delight transferred to the shopkeepers, who looked forward to their visits each morning.

To-To had never been treated so well and reveled in it. Her appreciation for the situation was enhanced by Om's presence, because it was common practice in commercial colonial cities for young children who went into public places without a chaperone to be seized and held for ransom. That was an easier way to accumulate funds than to work. Any move toward the two girls would bring down a horde of women against the cretin. Once they finished with him, Om would be waiting.

The girls asked about the availability of cosmetics and were directed to merchants who purveyed goods from the Far East. Moe provided the girls with a supply of the expensive cosmetics as well as a piece of jade for each. He brought more such supplies for the people back home.

Nefertiti, who was ten-years old, approached him and placed her hand on his arm, waiting for his attention, which he gave slowly, knowing what was coming.

"You are one of the most-valuable citizens in our colony. Don't present any gifts of these treasures to any woman except me or To-To, or you'll find a husband at your door with a spear."

He smiled fondly and nodded, recognizing the value of her concern. "I'll never fail you, Princess."

Nefertiti made a special trip to the square to buy honey for the oasis. Young Iberian women floated past Om's nose in their best clothing without his noticing. To-To noticed, though, and she realized she had to be ready for him soon, or she'd lose her chance.

Some wondered how Moe had so much generosity for so many and still had a stack of Roman coins available when needed. The solution was simple—he stole them.

Thirteen

On the second day of the girls' shopping spree, two Roman cargo ships appeared on the horizon. Moe checked that Om knew, then went to the Viking ships and chatted with their commanders. He imparted his knowledge of Roman ships and tactics to them, then he suggested a plan that made them grin.

They sailed after the two ships and caught them, lashing them together and plundering their cargo. When the ships were emptied, they were allowed to go ashore and break up on the rocks.

The Vikings returned to the town and left 10% of the booty in the marketplace for the women to fight over. They would be welcomed when they returned.

The rest of the treasure went north where the sailors were the biggest heroes in years. They were expected to brag about their adventure and return the following summer, perhaps with more ships, to keep the balance of power from swinging too far in the Romans' favor.

Why steal from honest landsmen as poor as themselves when Moe taught them how to take booty from fat Roman cargo ships?

Nefertiti and To-To sensed Moe was about to complete his commissioning for the voyage home and made their own plans. He was most vulnerable in the evening before a fire, when they enveloped him. They could control a man who loved them unless they made a mistake and allowed him to wake up. Nefertiti was a princess, but the children were entrusted in his care, and he wouldn't fail such a trust.

They suggested he make a slight detour on the way home to visit a place called Ostia.

Om woke up.

Fourteen

Ostia was a useless mud flat, but it was snuggled up right under Rome's nose only ten miles away. Moe wanted answers.

Nefertiti explained she learned a lot about medicine from Ooze but learned about other plants and herbs that existed elsewhere. She also learned about compounding mixtures using a mortar and pestle. A medicine woman, considered insane, a sorceress, or oldest, most-knowledgeable of medicine women lived in Ostia. If her trip was to gain her as much as possible, she had to visit Ostia.

Nefertiti was prepared, knowing Moe was already considering the problem. He would deny her nothing, especially for a worthy goal, but she wasn't just his princess and the princess of the Phoenicians. She was also the princess of the Egyptians. She had to return safely from her journey. Her proposal was a very hazardous voyage for a single ship.

The more Moe thought about it, the more he realized such a trip wasn't quite as dangerous as he first assumed. Cargo ships might pass near them, but the Roman navy was stationed on the east coast and areas even farther east. The Romans had no enemies to the west and ignored that direction. Cargo ships didn't stand in toward Ostia, because it was too shallow, and there were no harbor facilities or stevedores. Rome was just uphill from Ostia, but the

Romans didn't import much from the sea, because Italy was a lush land of plenty.

Then there were the Vikings, who might enjoy a little combat with a clumsy Roman round ship if the chance came. Why not?

Arrangements were swiftly made. The three ships sailed for Ostia to visit an ancient crone of at least eighty years in a time when people rarely lived past forty.

Moe proceeded inshore, taking careful soundings on the way. It was local low tide, and the stink of exposed sea bottom quickly replaced the fresh sea air. After the huts were carefully investigated, Om and the girls went to pay their respects.

The Ancient One was less than enchanted by their presence. After several hours of the girls intelligently discussing medicine, her reticence cracked, and she gradually joined in. As hoped, she was a treasure trove of knowledge. She not only gave the girls a healthy supply of unknown plants and herbs but also potions made from them, which had earned her the reputation of a witch and seer. She taught the girls how to make and use those preparations. To-To kept the information to herself and eventually earned a reputation as a magician and mystic, while Nefertiti taught all who sought to learn the medical arts.

The Old One added enormously to their knowledge of herbs used in cooking, too. It was no wonder the Romans were such hedonists.

She added a bit of lore they hadn't heard—medicine men and women were bound to all gods and goddesses by oath not to bring harm to their patients. Centuries later, that would become the Hippocratic Oath, without mention of any deities.

Moe used the hours to sound the approaches to Ostia at high tide, hoping the knowledge would become useful some day.

After picking up Om and the girls, Moe sailed from Ostia to join the Vikings. They had already taken a fat merchant ship on its way to resupply a Roman outpost and were in high spirits. They thanked Moe for inviting them along for a possible fight with a bireme and for the great tale they would have to tell about tweaking Rome right under its nose. He thanked them for the escort, agreed to meet them on the Iberian coast in spring, and watched them sail toward home.

When they returned to the coastal colony, Nefertiti saw Moori waiting, hitched to a new cart with a beautiful floral garland around her neck. She ran down the gangplank and hugged Moori, as she nuzzled her in return. When the cart was ready to leave for the oasis, Nefertiti jumped up onto the cart bed and took the reins to enjoy the pleasure of driving her new toy. Local boys thought Amun would drive, sitting as usual right behind Moori, so they deliberately gave the pony a lot of fresh, green grass.

When Nefertiti asked Moori to trot, she quickly received the gift intended to Amun. Though speckled, she retained her poise and ordered Amun to walk the pony, then start again with him driving. She asked him to meet her at Atli's hut when they reached the oasis. The sense of dread they left behind was thick in the air, but no one stepped forward to save Amun.

While cleaning Nefertiti, To-To explained the trick and added it was intended for Amun, not for the princess. The garland was woven by Amun to place on Moori as a way of pleasing Nefertiti.

At the oasis, Nefertiti and Amun went directly to Atli's hut, although, as she expected, he wasn't there. She quickly explained she would visit a spot on the outer edge of the oasis to the southwest she knew about. It had good grazing for Moori, which provided an excuse, and Morg would be drinking his vat of beer in a nearby cemetery at that time of day, which would deter anyone from the oasis. Besides, Om was only twenty meters away at any time, so it had to be safe.

Amun armed himself anyway. Moori would be able to sense a stranger from far away. Nefertiti's plan was good.

They walked the vale beyond the graveyard hand-in-hand, and she laughed aloud and happily. As they talked, they learned much of each other. They even finished each other's sentences. They weren't being rude, just enmeshed in their private conspiracy, the princess and the stable boy. They lay in the tall grass and made up stories about the pictures they saw in the clouds, one adding to the other's story until the tale was told.

Neither had been formally educated, yet both were intelligent and had absorbed much. They took great pleasure in teaching each other. Amun taught her a game where two circles were drawn in the sand, one inside the other. A stone tossed from behind a line drawn three paces away and resting against either circle gave points, while a stone tossed between the circles earned nothing. If the stone landed outside the largest circle, it subtracted points. That game often entertained crowds.

They practiced arithmetic, too. In a society based on trade and commerce, arithmetic was essential, where language skills weren't. Polyglot would do.

Amun told her how he was concerned for her safety the entire time she was away. After all, she was in a single ship on the sea. The danger wasn't just from enemy warships. There were also storms, tsunamis, and volcanic eruptions. Keenly feeling his inability to protect her, he felt frustrated.

Nefertiti didn't interrupt him. He told her how much he loved her and thought of her all the time. She treasured both interpretations of his words and didn't want to interrupt him for anything.

He assured her he would build a dashboard for the cart. He drew it in the sand in elaborate detail, seeking her approval, which she quickly gave. It also gave the impression he was being punished, albeit leniently, to everyone's relief.

Om stood alertly at guard, ready for the approach of anyone, friend or foe. He hoped to ease the young couple back to reality.

Moori shared the vigil with him, enjoying the magical quality of that quiet place, filled with bird song and sweet grass. She hoped she'd be invited back.

Fifteen

Ooze was in bad physical health, although she was mentally acute. She was delighted to see the girls safely home and was entranced with the foreign herbs and plants. The idea of making potions was mind-boggling. She'd never considered making them before. She agreed with Nefertiti that they should spend the winter studying everything available from the trips to Iberia and Ostia.

It occurred to Nefertiti that she and To-To might be the only people in the world with so much knowledge of medicine. At that time, surgery was the sole province of the Egyptians.

She went to Moe and asked that she and To-To be allowed to accompany him back to Iberia in the spring. After that, she wanted to visit the Nile and hoped the Vikings would accompany them to avoid any interruptions to their trip. She wanted the Egyptians to be told in advance that the Vikings were there with her and would enjoy ridding her of any Romans who might arrive. They wouldn't be allowed to interfere with commerce or enter the harbor.

Moe heard something new in Nefertiti's voice. She was being tactful but commanding. He agreed to her request.

After dark on an early spring evening, Moe set sail for Iberia. He wanted to be well out of sight of any landmass by morning. He planned to cross several commercial sea lanes in the early morning mist and be over the visible horizon from them by sunrise.

He hove to on a line between the Pillars of Hercules and Marbella, then waited for the Vikings. When he saw them in the night, they sailed into the port together.

The townsfolk erupted with joy and anticipation. Three women Moe knew well met him at the dock, warning him there were strange men in town who shared a common cause. They knew one of the girls was Nefertiti and wanted to abduct her for ransom.

Moe sent Nefertiti into town to offer her wealth of medical knowledge, accompanying her with Om and six sailors armed for battle as infantry. Each man held a short, wicked scimitar designed for parrying a spear thrust and gutting the soldier by charging in close, inside the spear's arc, and striking below the skirt of his body armor.

When the Vikings saw a fight brewing, they came boiling over the gunwales and hurried to assist. Their commanders warned them that Moe was a friend who made them rich and famous, so they would need some finesse. The Vikings agreed to blend in and be ready.

There was little hope the Vikings would be able to blend in, but their wide smiles and joyful anticipation were the only cloak the girls needed.

The two shipwrights, produced as promised the previous fall, absorbed everything about the two ship types in a fraction of the time their commanders needed. They were astonished at the way ship builders from two different worlds arrived at nearly identical solutions to naval design.

The Vikings built their ships slightly smaller but much tougher. They had to survive deep fjords and challenge the Atlantic Ocean. Accordingly, they were clinker built, with staves overlapping from gunwale to keel. Water smashing against the boat was directed down to the sea. Calk could be added from inside in any volume to keep the ship dry. The sailors stowed their spears inside the gunnels where they sat to row. When the oars were shipped, they were piled down the centerline to be out of the way during battle. They had a single square sail, good for power when the wind was right but useless when it wasn't. Then they needed muscle and oars.

The Viking ships were made of spruce, while the Phoenicians used cedar. The Viking prow was carved into a fierce dragon, while a Phoenician ship's prow was whatever the owner wanted. Moe had an asp on his prow, an Egyptian cobra that looked aft, not forward, waiting for the right moment to turn and strike.

Moe's ship wasn't typical of other Phoenician ships. All were commercial vessels except his, which was a warship, because he had to protect the princess successfully. Losing her was intolerable.

Accordingly, the ship was delicate, able to flee any opponent, float in shallows, or sail well before the wind. Her strakes were mated one to the next and bound together with two tiny holes through which rawhide was tied, which would tighten over time. At construction, tourniquets were used to draw the wood into a single entity. By the time Kufu built his pyramid, he chose a forerunner of Moe's design and took it into history with him.

Moe visited the Vikings to discuss a plan. The captains were both drunk on mead, but they wanted to hear Moe's thoughts. He was a clever devil who was never wrong.

When they asked if morning would be too late for their discussion, Moe laughed and said, "Your shipwrights will fight to keep their boats for a few more days. Morning will do."

"Mead can sometimes change from a friend to a wretched foe by morning," one captain said.

"My princess will have you fully alert if you need it, though I doubt you'll enjoy the cure."

"We'll obey her and will be ready to listen to you tomorrow, even if it's on our knees."

Moe sat on a rock on the beach, enjoying the morning and eating a few clams, when the Vikings joined him. He grinned and asked, "How are your heads?"

They grinned back ruefully.

"What is mead, anyway?"

"We don't know how it is made, but in the spring when bees seek out new blossoms to extract nectar to make honey, men more courageous than ourselves steal the honey, ferment it, and add a little water. Such a potion makes winter burst into spring, thaws ice, and sets the stage of battle."

Hearing the reference to a potion, Moe made a note to tell Nefertiti about it.

While eating clams, the three men began discussing a plan of action.

"Would you like to plunder two Roman round ships in the first three days you're here and spend the rest of the summer in comfort in Iberia? You'll arrive home as heroes with no questions asked. Or you can spend all your time seeking combat."

They grinned at him.

"I can promise a fight."

They hugged him like brothers, with Nefertiti their little sister.

Sixteen

Moe suggested they sail to Ostia in company. He learned that two Roman biremes escorting two round ships were expecting him. He planned to show himself, then flee south with the north wind behind him. The biremes would follow, leaving the round ships as easy targets for the Vikings, who would lurk just over the horizon. They would lash the two ships together and anchor them in shallow water, then sail rapidly south before the north wind.

The plan worked, and the Roman biremes were sunk with all hands, mostly slaves. After rowing north against the wind to Ostia, they delivered the two round ships to be plundered. The Vikings told the villagers to plunder the ships quickly, then scuttle them in deep water to the north. The villagers got several years' worth of grain and wine, while the Vikings reaped a harvest of small, light valuables and the gratitude of the locals.

As they sailed, some of the men grumbled about leaving the wine behind, but Moe reminded them that Roman wine was no good, while Roman women were thick and short. Iberian wine was superb, and the women were incomparable.

When they arrived back in Marbella, they were greeted by the news that every stone that could he tapped with a chisel had been turned into a bust of Nefertiti as a chubby infant with huge black circles around her eyes and gleaming red cheeks. When it became known that the young visitor of the previous year was actually Nefertiti, an industry formed to create those busts for the sale of cosmetics, and that continued for hundreds of years. Nefertiti was as beautiful as a child as she was as a woman.

Moe left Marbella on the tide early in the morning, tacking ship against the Saharan winds blowing north at that time of year. He wanted to join a Phoenician trading convoy traveling from west to east on a long, comfortable broad reach. That would bring him to an island nation on the trade route at a crossroads of trade. That island southeast of Sicily allowed the islanders to sample and acquire art, foods, and customs from many nations. They were a fortunate people who made the most of their situation.

Moe wanted the girls to visit and learn before taking them back to the Nile. The lush island had a mountainous interior. As they approached, they saw two harbors filled with commercial traffic. Moe warned the girls that warships were allowed only two days to visit, so they had to get busy.

The harbor they entered was extensively decorated with colorful designs. Streets led away from the harbor for carts, and the buildings lining the streets were colorful, too. A short excursion revealed that color was everywhere, even on interior walls. The place was the envy of all visitors, and the island also possessed a standing army bigger than that of Rome, Athens, or Egypt. It was called Atlantis.

A courier approached, bowed deeply, and presented a document to Nefertiti. It was an invitation for her and her attendants to visit the palace.

She agreed, and they were led to the residence behind the town and above the harbor with a breathtaking view.

The royal family consisted of King Heron, his wives, Lido and Alie, and their sons, Petro, Hugo, and Denis. The boys had been warned a foreign dignitary was visiting, so they should dress accordingly. They protested, but then complied.

Nefertiti walked between rows of columns, followed by Lady To-To. The stunned boys realized such a beautiful young woman could only be Nefertiti. They felt that the four most beautiful women in the world were in the same room with them and wished they dressed even better.

Nefertiti received a tour of the residence and again saw an insistence on color, predominantly orange. The columns were decorated with dancing women and graceful animals, without any bullocks. The bed chambers were white, with tall windows facing north and south to take advantage of the prevailing winds during the two main seasons.

The huge staff immediately began planning a feast for Nefertiti. Place settings consisted of spoons, three-tined forks, and spatulas. When To-To saw that, she took a scalpel from her kit and placed it at Nefertiti's right hand. Nefertiti smiled her thanks, because she wasn't armed with a dagger. It was in that time and place that modern settings began to evolve.

The feast consisted of eight courses, all superb and small in honor of Nefertiti's diminutive size. The two boys could have eaten triple servings, like all growing boys, but they patiently waited to join Om, To-To, and the staff in the kitchen. Petro, who was thoroughly bewitched, played with his food and hung on Nefertiti's every word.

Afterward, Nefertiti, To-To, Om, and Petro, along with two soldiers, set out to tour the town. Om saw everyone wore colorful clothing, then he saw six people in colorless sailor's clothing in an alley. Om indicated their presence to the others, and they quickly prepared.

When the abductors came out, they were met with four spear points. To-To leaped to Om's opponent, placed her foot on the man's chest, and tore the obsidian point from his throat. Om had his javelin in hand again before he could draw his sword.

Petro was impressed.

The remaining sailors told Om of their captain's orders to abduct Nefertiti, and Petro immediately sent word to his father of the violation of the port's courtesy and his threat to the houses of the king and the Pharaoh. The captain would be executed before sunset, while the fate of his crew would be left to the statesmen.

The king sent a messenger back to Petro advising him to use his discretion whether the party would continue to the ancient ruins on the northwest shore or would return to his residence. The king ordered a military exercise to take place above the old natural harbor. If any ship was sighted making for that place, it would be ambushed.

Petro explained the alternatives, and the girls said they didn't want the captain's greed to ruin their day. They still wanted to see the ruins. Besides, they were traveling in a warship that had to leave in the morning.

Petro sent messages to his father and Moe, then led the way to the beach. The girls kicked off their sandals and luxuriated in the pure, shell-free sand. All their senses were indulged. The Mediterranean Sea pawed at the beach, then faded from green to blue in the distance under a clear azure sky. The artesian springs along the way put their oasis to shame.

Om saw the armed escort, and so did To-To, who felt grateful. She was serious in her duty to protect Nefertiti. She was serious about Om, too, and didn't want him to require any medical assistance in such a paradise.

The ruins still retained some of the color and art of the ancient ones. Nefertiti pursued some of the artifacts into grottos off the harbor, while Petro pursued her. He was a good, well-motivated guide. Seeing her interest in color, he asked if she liked flowers.

She did, and Petro engaged her in conversation for his next move. He gestured toward the shore, and she saw masses of white blossoms with colorful birds among them. She was enchanted, and he was enchanted with her.

Though he'd been holding his breath in rapt admiration, he found the wit to say, "No. Closer."

She saw a patch of green on a wharf piling. As they approached the moss, he said, "Look closely."

When she did, she shook her head in confusion.

"Look for tiny red blossoms."

When she saw them, she laughed in delight and smiled at him. Her smile was rare and almost never seen, but that day, he saw it.

"I can give you some of the white flowers now, but they'd die at sea on your way to Egypt. The red flowers must remain here in their natural environment. You must come see them again."

She understood his meaning. If she nodded, she could have two lovers and a future Pharaoh, but what then?

She sat on the pier dangling her toes in the water.

"Some of the fish here have teeth," he said. "They would enjoy your toes as much as I do."

She quickly withdrew her feet and pulled on her sandals. On the way back, she ran in the surf and dared the fish to crawl onto the sand for a nibble.

Her armed guard watched her carefully from their positions of concealment. They would be expected to tell their wives every detail of what she wore, what she said, and how she treated others. All the men loved her and would have signed up en masse to be her bodyguards. That would please the women. The fact that none of them mentioned Lady To-To would sink in later.

When the party returned to the royal residence, they found Petro had arranged with the king for the ship to remain in the harbor for an additional day. The queens would take the girls shopping in one of the best town squares in the morning.

Petro didn't wait until morning. As soon as Nefertiti and To-To retired to their room, he climbed the vines to the balcony. They greeted him with helping hands and laughter. To-To excused herself to her room. As she entered the hall through the door, she assured Om all was well, and he understood what she meant.

Petro stayed until the moon rose and extended its path across the sea to the balcony, then he left as he arrived. His presence lingered, and neither Nefertiti nor To-To slept.

Petro found the king waiting for him in the front hall, amused. He hadn't realized he could be seen climbing the vines. They talked, and Petro slowly understood what a burden of decision he was imposing in Nefertiti. Perhaps she would be wise just to make no decision.

In midmorning, Nefertiti visited the town square with the queens. The women of the city completed their daily food shopping hours earlier but returned for a chance to see Nefertiti. She didn't disappoint. She wore a simple, gleaming white gown, elegant and riveting in a throng of such colorful people with their many colored adornments. She wore her tiny tiara.

The people were noisy and happy, and Nefertiti was serene and pleased. She deliberately walked through the crowd to be as close to as many as possible.

The queens mounted stairs where they could overlook the square and conspire about how Nefertiti might be induced to stay with Petro. Their island would become the crossroads of the world.

Petro thought along the same lines, with himself as the crossroads and Nefertiti the traffic. The women in the square wanted Nefertiti, too, but they weren't so certain they wanted Lady To-To to stay on their island with the men.

Seventeen

Princess Elvira of the Hittites arrived on the island kingdom that morning, supposedly on a trading mission for her father, the king. Actually, she intended to snag Prince Petro for herself. She had no thought of failure, being unable to imagine any competitor as beautiful as she. Hittite princes outdid themselves daily to earn her regard through charm and poetry. Elvira accepted their praise but knew she deserved more. Her self-regard was boundless.

Elvira detached herself from that line of thought with difficulty and listened to conversation in the square. It seemed the Egyptian princess had arrived first and already had her hooks so deeply into Petro that the people expected Nefertiti to become their princess and eventually their queen. They liked the idea, too.

Elvira sent a messenger to the royal residence to announce her arrival and say she looked forward to staying with the family for a few days. It was a tactless expectation, but it was allowed to pass. After all, the Hittites were known to be tactless. They couldn't be instructed in the art of tact any more than a great cat could be tamed.

Elvira arrived at the residence with a squad of armed troops and retinue of ladies in waiting. The commander of the royal guard thanked the squad leader for escorting the princess and sent him and his squad, along with half the retinue, back to the ship with the promise to be personally responsible for the princess' safety. He relieved the princess of her spear and sword but didn't ask for her dagger, since ladies of royal rank kept those by protocol. Besides, she would need it if a meat dish was served.

Once settled into her rooms, Elvira went directly to Nefertiti's quarters, where she introduced herself and declared that Nefertiti preceding her made no difference in the outcome. Petro would be hers. Nefertiti was wasting her time.

Elvira seemed like an apparition to Nefertiti. Her fan of red hair stood out around her head, and her eyes were violet. Her skin was white, something Nefertiti hadn't seen before, although she heard of it. The Vikings she met were sailors with healthy tans. Elvira had a good face and figure, but her aura was arrogant and menacing. Nefertiti didn't see her as the beauty she assumed she was, although she was striking and certainly formidable.

She treated Elvira gently, realizing that life to the Hittites was a war game of thrust and parry, whether on the battlefield with arms or in conversation within the royal residence. She explained she stopped at the island as a normal part of her visit to the Nile. She knew nothing of Petro's existence in advance and would depart in the morning, because she was traveling in a warship. She didn't expect to return.

Elvira was free to compete for Petro's affection, but Nefertiti advised her that it was all moot. The fates of royal children were decided by their fathers, including the king of Atlantis, Elvira's father, and Nefertiti's Pharaoh of Egypt. Queens, sons, and daughters had some input, but the decision belonged to the king.

Elvira was deflated, something that was new to her, as a serene Nefertiti explained the reality of the world without rancor, using barely two dozen words. The best tactic for Elvira was retreat.

Besides, she knew that both Om and To-To stood ready to defend their charge, something Elvira could approve of.

The two princesses realized the best thing was to become girl-friends. They may need that friendship someday. With amusement, they agreed they came from harsh environments, were meeting for the first time in paradise, and should spend the time enjoying it.

When the two princesses parted company for the evening, each formulated a plan for the morning. Elvira thought the Egyptians would be leaving, since their time of welcome had expired. She didn't know the king extended their stay.

She sent for her commander and instructed him to allow the Egyptians to be hull down over the horizon before he left the harbor, then follow discretely to keep their mast in view. He was told to ensure that Nefertiti didn't reverse course and start another two-day visit with Petro. Above all, he was to make sure she boarded the ship and sailed away.

Nefertiti, who expected something like that from Elvira, sent for Moe. Together, they hatched a plan to embarrass Elvira in a way that she couldn't speak of it.

When Moe left the residence, Nefertiti went to meet the two queens, who gleefully joined in the deception. She needed two girls to act as stand-ins for her and To-To on a secret mission. They had to be volunteers, since there was the potential for danger, and in each case, the families had to consent.

There was no problem. In fact, the problem would be to keep the plan secret for the one day it required. Nefertiti's selection of the two girls resulted in something they always dreamed. Their mothers' social status went up a notch overnight.

In early morning, the Egyptian warship left under oar power with two ladies aboard in boat cloaks. Moe didn't step his mast, because the wind blew from the south. He didn't want Kurt, the Hittite commander, to be able to follow him by sighting on his mast.

Soon, Kurt would realize something was afoot. He was a clever commander and was on Moe's list of possible commanders in the future Egyptian navy. Kurt was a mercenary sailor who would have no trouble changing allegiances.

Moe continued south until he met a small storm. He circled it to the south, then stepped his mast and took a reciprocal course under sail back toward Atlantis, following the storm. He gave command to Solomon, his first officer, a fine sailor of Lebanese extraction, another one of Moe's list of possible future commanders. He wanted to see how Solomon handled the situation.

When the princess' clumsy barge finally emerged from the storm, Solomon rushed in under sail and snapped the ship with grappling hooks. The crew had no time to ship oars and retrieve their spears.

As the two ships rode easily side-by-side, Moe and Kurt grinned at each other. Moe's deception had saved lives. Kurt also noted that Solomon was the one to execute the move.

"Would you prefer a stormy day at sea or a day with Elvira?" Moe asked Kurt.

"I love an ugly day on the Mediterranean and the sting of spray on my face," Kurt replied, not wishing to invite death unless it was time of war.

The Hittite princess laid a trap for Nefertiti, who sprung it. The Egyptian fox outwitted the Hittite fox. If her father learned of such a gross misuse of the royal barge, he might never let her use it again.

The king of Atlantis had no daughters and would be pleased to welcome Nefertiti into his household. The problem was, the Pharaoh felt the same way.

That night, after all were asleep, the king and his queens discussed the matter. He knew his son was smitten with Nefertiti, and the queens agreed she returned his regard. However, Nefertiti had something on her mind, probably her indebtedness to the Pharaoh.

The king decided to send his most-trusted emissary to Egypt to speak with the Pharaoh's old friend and advisor. It would be an exploratory talk. There was no need to set up anyone for a fall.

In the morning, the king sent for his emissary and explained that the Egyptian princess had Petro under her spell and could lead him anywhere by the nose. The emissary agreed she could lead anyone in the nation wherever she chose.

The emissary explained Om's total loyalty to Nefertiti and whatever she chose. Lady To-To was the same.

"Where did Nefertiti stand during the confrontation with the squad of sailors?" the king asked.

"She was directly behind Petro, with To-To behind Om. The men were shoulder to shoulder. After the business was finished, Om nodded his approval of Petro."

"Proceed to Egypt and confer with the Pharaoh's advisor. Tactfully explain the future Pharaoh's shortcomings, then mention Petro's manliness, courage, and command. Nefertiti would still marry royalty and would remain in a class by herself. Seeing the couple together would bring the admiration and allegiance of the known world. The Pharaoh must see that dark vision of the future must be tempered. Nefertiti would be happy here. Akhenaton need not feel too aggrieved, because his first wife, Kiya, still lives and has given him Tut and Nebnefer. The Pharaoh can take credit for it all."

The plan would ultimately fail, but Nefertiti and Petro would at least know they tried.

Eighteen

Mut, Nefertiti's younger sister by two years, uncomfortably awaited her arrival at the Nile. She had only the vaguest memory of Nefertiti but had heard many stories. People said Nefertiti would conquer Egypt with its full consent. Mut would have to share her toys with her sister, who was still a child, and she was jealous and didn't want that. She already had the admiration of every boy and man, and she treasured that. It didn't matter that Nefertiti was unavailable to them, nor did it matter that even women loved her.

Mut dreaded being set aside. She was even more uncomfortable knowing that such thinking wasn't reasonable. Hopes that Nefertiti's ship would sink weren't to be tolerated, no matter how often they returned. She was no longer a child, and that was the problem.

Mut vowed to be gracious and helpful, as a younger sister should. She packed her best gowns for a short trip to the Nile and personally buffed her jewelry, wondering if the salty sea breeze would tarnish Nefertiti's trinkets.

Nineteen

Upon her arrival at the Nile, Nefertiti was met by her younger sister, Mut. Mut showed instant evidence of the difference between the culture of the oasis and that of the modern cities of Egypt. She was dripping with jewelry, including a ceremonial dagger at her girdle, and was accompanied by two ladies in waiting and four soldiers. In view of all that jewelry, the soldiers seemed a prudent escort.

Mutnodjmet proved a fine guide to Egypt and its history. They visited cities and towns on the delta, and Nefertiti was received in all places with happy adulation. She was the best-known and most-revered woman in Egypt based on the rumors and stories from sailors and soldiers.

She did nothing to disappoint the people. She walked with an erect royal carriage. Her chin was slightly lifted, but her eyes addressed each person individually. The soldiers saluted her, artisans acknowledged her, and women ambushed her as much as they dared. Among them was a queen, Nefertiti of Egypt, and she was theirs.

Then there was Om. Women saw a young god, bronzed and beautiful, who was always at Nefertiti's side. Many envied such devotion and would have diverted it toward themselves if they dared.

The men, however, saw Om as death personified. Legend had it that he left no living opponent behind, and it was probably true. Atli thought that was part of his doctrine. Legend further declaimed that if Om lifted his javelin toward an enemy, and he saw the sparkle of sunlight on the spear point, he was a dead man. Rumor built legend, and legend built reputation. A corps stood where Om stood.

Mut arranged for a royal barge to take the girls and a retinue for a tour of the upper Nile. There they saw the marvels of the recent past and evidence from ancient times. Why allow those earlier works to be covered in sand?

On the return journey north, Nefertiti asked to visit Aktmim on the east bank, where it was said she was born. There were divided opinions about her being born there, since her parents were ambassadors who traveled almost constantly. Nefertiti thought she might remember something.

An emissary went ahead to make arrangements. When they arrived, it was late evening. They were fourteen miles from the city but were assured it was an easy trip, and the royal accommodations weren't currently in use. Three carts and two soldiers awaited them, as well as provisions for the company's comfort. Setting off at a brisk pace, they arrived at dusk. Aktmim, known as a lively town with a reputation for free trade, appeared deserted.

Om brought the little caravan to a halt 100 meters before the low wall and studied it. The gates were open but unmanned. No dust drifted on the air. Nefertiti, aware of Om's caution, stood beside him to see what he saw. The provisions were for a trip intended to arrive at night, yet there were no torches and no means to light any. There was water but no food, only two soldiers. Four were provided to meet Nefertiti at the royal facilities on the Nile.

Om and Nefertiti smelled a trap, although it wasn't planned by a military man. There was no need for food or torches if they were intended to be slain, and it was better to sacrifice two soldiers rather than waste four more. Leaving such clear clues was a deadly mistake. It was apparent that no one bothered to tell the assassins that they faced Om.

As Om stepped onto the road, Nefertiti joined him on his left side, her hand resting on his forearm. The two soldiers stood on their flanks. As they crested a low dune, Om raised his javelin high and let the last rays of the setting sun ripple on the obsidian point. The battle was already over.

The two soldiers accompanying Om hadn't met before, but they looked at each other and both realized they'd been sent on that detail to be sacrificed. Someone was using them as superficial dressing. They saw Om walking toward battle with his queen at his side, and his reputation firmly embedded in his opponents' imaginations. The assassins elected to depart in silent haste. By morning, they were so deep into the Sahara, not even buzzards flew in the sky.

The two soldiers fell into step with Om and Nefertiti. Mut, feeling grudging respect for her big sister, knew the tale of this moment would race north and south along the Nile. As she watched them approach the town together, she paid special attention to Om and Nefertiti together and thought, *Uh-huh.*

Twenty

Nefertiti and Om held a council of war. It wasn't an attempted abduction, because she was no longer a child. She was the soon-to-be queen of Egypt. It was a planned assassination and the murder of everyone who witnessed it. That meant no one in the caravan was part of the plan. The assassins were nomads, which mean they weren't hired by the army. Civil servants wouldn't have used nomads, either. A foreign country would have no motive for assassination. The nomads hadn't planned it to enrich themselves, because they were willing to steal everything in Egypt and would do so at any moment.

Was it the work of Princess Elvira? Nefertiti rejected the thought. That wasn't her way.

Other princesses who would be queen had no reason to attack Nefertiti, because she had to be of age to become eligible to marry. Was the plot directed against someone else in the caravan? Had Mut enraged someone? Was it jealousy? Did someone think he could get at Akhenaton by killing his future wife? What about the clergy, who many suspected of murdering her parents? If Akhenaton carried out his plans once he was Pharaoh, the clergy would be out of work and would have to look for honest employment, which they would consider a disaster.

As a polytheistic country, Egypt's deities each had its own separate clergy, each of which expected ten percent of all a worshipper possessed. Akhenaton wasn't the first to see merit in ridding the country of clerics and worship only one god. That gave the clerics a good motive for murder. Their wives were even more dangerous. Anyone who believed that such religious folk would accept the loss meekly was also someone who believed it was safe to walk on a carpet of asps. No Pharaoh had ever issued such a decree, so there hadn't been a need to take action to preserve the *status quo ante*.

Egypt stood upon three pillars—the Pharaoh, the army, and the clergy. The Pharaoh was the head of the royal family, regardless of age. He appointed himself a god equal to all others and had his likeness sculpted with the grandest of them, chatting amicably. He was always the top soldier no matter how inept he might be. Since there was no standing army, he appointed general liberally, because they had no troops to mislead. There was a palace guard, but they weren't even issued spears, because they might hurt someone.

Egypt was proving to be a far more dangerous place than the oasis. Nefertiti thought she should have an ornamental dagger made for herself, except the blade would be military grade. Om held out his hand to comfort her, and she came into his arms.

Later, after they were settled in the royal accommodations, Mut went to Nefertiti's room and announced that the little show outside the walls was but a preview of what was to come.

"We exist in the royal history of Egypt," Mut said. "Those who aren't in that history exist in the larger purview of the history of mankind. Both histories are soaked in blood, but they differ significantly.

"These differences can be illustrated by thinking of certain animal species all Egyptians know. The praying mantis emerges from its egg and is immediately ready to eat the head of his brother doing the same. Cannibalism doesn't even enter into it. The defensive tactic of choice for them is to take a position equally distant from all their kin and shift to keep that position when one of the others shifts. Their weapon is a set of massive claws.

"The honey bee emerges into the light of day to see her sister doing the same and goes to assist her. They tumble over each other when performing their communal tasks. Their weapons are defensive and remain sheathed for life or until needed.

"Our own parents were assassinated in a crime that was never solved. That act was meant to achieve an end. To this day, no one is certain what the desired result was. No one took their positions as ambassadors, and no foreign country seemed to benefit from their deaths."

Mut seemed inclined to talk. She went to a comfortable stool and sat down. Her garment had all the colors of the rainbow, topped off with a dead scarab beetle as her brooch. It gleamed with iridescence, but it was still just a dung beetle. Nefertiti didn't like the insect even when it was portrayed in stone by a skilled artisan. Still, she sensed that Mut thought she was on a mission.

Mut felt that Nefertiti couldn't have learned the art of diplomacy while sitting at an oasis, while Mut survived many encounters in the court on the Nile. In truth, Nefertiti was adept at diplomacy and already had the trust and confidence of most of the known world. What Mut meant to impart was the art of palace in-fighting. Nefertiti didn't need her advice, having already won that battle more than once. However, Mut might have a nugget or two of information, and Nefertiti never ignored the chance to tap a reliable source. Mut was as much an enigma to her as the other members of the court. Potentially, Mut was the most dangerous of them all. While Mut wove her tale, Nefertiti remained serene and attentive.

"All ranks in Egypt have names that are almost a meter long," Mut said. "Those ranks refer to the person's heredity and mental and physical attributes in eloquent terms reserved for royalty, even before a babe is born. People reduce their names to a manageable length unless he becomes Pharaoh, whereupon the entire name is restored and rendered in stone.

"Kai is one to watch. She is the most-evil person in our extended family. When she was born, she seized her mother's amulet and cried when it was taken from her, indicating her rightful ownership. She grew proficient as a thief and liar. If she visits you in your quarters, you can't ever leave her alone, because she'll steal your stove, then return for the smoke.

"Her natural preference is to lie rather than acknowledge the truth. The only exception seems to be when the lie requires such an elaborate deception that she would be hard-pressed to remember it later."

Mut spent time elaborating on Kai's deficiencies. She added that all the other family members were guilty of the same conduct though not to the same degree. They were like a nest of newly hatched praying mantises, adjusting their positions when anyone moved.

There was really no cause for such scheming. Nefertiti and Pharaoh made careful precautions against family schemes.

The princesses were equally venomous, except that Kai backed her venom with the best female attributes. The princes were equally insipid since they had no way to employ their talents. Even commoners were more interesting, since they worked three or four days each week, with the remainder of their time their own.

Assassinations within the royal family occurred at an average of two per generation. They were always done by proxy, because the penalty for being caught was public execution. Mut assured

Nefertiti that she was under the Pharaoh's personal protection. Besides, when she arrived, she brought an entire cadre from the oasis, and they were more dedicated to her than to Egypt itself.

There was Om, too. Mut observed that commoners weren't publicly executed. They were killed on the spot without any form of appeal and without any offer of imprisonment as an alternative. There were no incarceration facilities in the country. It was a purely administrative matter.

"What have you been taught about female Pharaohs in the past?" Nefertiti asked.

Mut knew where that question was leading. There had been two in history. "My teachers didn't know the name of the first, but the second was Hatsupshut. Both appeared at a time when Egypt needed a strong hand on the helm, and each did well. After the death of the first Pharaoh, men removed her visage from statues with heavy hammers. After the death of the second, they couldn't do it, because her likeness was carved into stone on the world's tallest obelisk, and no one could scale it. It still remains in place, with her face showing pasted-on whiskers for all to see."

Mut paused. "The matter of your ascension as Pharaoh has already been discussed. There are two routes for you. Your husband can seat you on the throne with him before he dies, or two men must die and you must have only daughters. In either case, that means the end of the Eighteenth Dynasty."

Mut stood and walked to the door. "A great explosion occurred at a granary this morning. A woman was killed, beheaded with her garment blown off her body. It was thought at first it might have been you, because the body had black pubic hair and a good figure, but that idea vanished when people observed you were never that well-endowed in life." With a merry laugh, she left.

Nefertiti persuaded Moe to visit the island one more time on their way home to the oasis. She knew she was letting herself in for a heartache that would last a lifetime. She had so enjoyed the riotous colors, vibrant life, art, and the people. She remembered Petro wading beside her ship with his wine cup raised to her as she left Atlantis.

"Do well what you are destined to do," he called.

Twenty-One

In the fall of her thirteenth year, Nefertiti set specific plans into motion. She spent hours in mature consultation with Atli, which she wouldn't have done earlier. She was no longer a child and needed the best insight she could get. As a member of royalty, at the age of fifteen, she was expected to marry royalty. Since that was her fate, she wanted to rise as high as she could, gaining the best situation possible.

Atli felt great sadness. He knew if he reached out, she would come into his arms as the child she once was, but that was no longer possible. Change was coming, and she turned to him for help, so he must be reliable at that time in her life.

He sent for To-To. When she arrived, he said, "Nefertiti has selected you as a permanent lady in waiting. Accordingly, you must begin training with weapons."

To-To was astonished. The only time she touched a weapon was to move it out of reach of a soldier who was a patient in the medical hut. No one had ever seen her astonished or serious about anything before.

When Atli explained why, she seemed to age into maturity instantly. A royal woman could be killed by her lady in waiting rather than suffer death or disgrace at the hand of another.

The following morning, Om provided her with a selection of throwing knives and asked her to experiment with them on the arms range until she felt familiar with them. They weren't daggers. Their weighted blades were attached to very light wood or bone-straight handles. When she selected the one she favored, Om began her training. She had a post as her target three meters away. It was close enough so she could be lethally effective but not so close that an alert soldier could take her weapon from her. She would have three knives under her skirt and was to practice until she could make the first appear as if by magic and fly from behind her ear in a straight, overhead arc, ending with her hand pointing directly where she looked.

Atli, judging her progress after a few weeks, was pleased. She was ready for the next two phases of her training. The first was psychological and tactical. The last was strength training. When the knife came out, it had to do what it was intended to do. Merely attracting the attention of her target by bouncing a knife off his chest would be suicide.

Atli walked the oasis with her. It was his experience that talk was more fruitful when walking than when at rest. Whether he was right about that for To-To was unknown, but she enjoyed his company. He told her that when she thought it prudent to go armed, she should think of everyone nearby as a threat to Nefertiti. If she knew she must use her weapons, it must be done instinctively and without losing the element of surprise. If she were in the infantry, he would have told her to use her spear without throwing it. Throwing a weapon meant the person was unarmed on the battlefield. After throwing a knife, she must instantly have her second knife in her hand to avoid being without a weapon.

He taught her the technique of closing her eyes and pointing her finger at the target post. When she opened her eyes, her finger should be aimed at the target. If not, she must shift her stance until she pointed at it.

As the people of the oasis became more accustomed to hearing knives thud into the post with increasing authority, the old saying about To-To as a child was resurrected—Do not come between To-To and her target.

During one of the walks with Atli, To-To confided she was increasingly interested in Om and thought of no one else.

"Is there any hope for me to be in his life?" she asked.

He pondered the question, because she deserved a straight answer. She was devoted to Nefertiti, and so was Om. Both were also devoted to Atli. Neither had any other interests. The elements were in place. It wasn't a question of what To-To should do but what she must not do. She must always be at his call and must not force the issue.

"Nefertiti will be queen someday, and she will want both of you available," Atli said. "Be careful about setting a trap for Om. He'll come to you."

Om went to visit Moe. When he pointed at his spear head, Moe nodded, and their communication was complete—on Moe's next trip, he needed to find suitable material for Om's javelins. Normally, Om left after such a brief conversation, but that day, he lingered.

Moe eyed him quizzically. OM signaled his interest in To-To, and Moe nodded.

"You'd better waste no time," Moe advised. "She's the tallest, strongest girl in the oasis. You and To-To will go with Nefertiti when the time comes. That timing is perfect for you, but it might also be perfect for other young men. You'd better ask Atli's permission to ask To-To to join with you. She can answer for herself, because she's an orphan, but if you get Atli involved, you'll be first among equals, without resorting to arms."

Om, thanking Moe for his advice, left. When he visited Atli and explained his interest in To-To, he survived the man's congratulatory blow to his shoulder.

Om met To-To at the medical hut and complained of a terrible headache that required her personal attention. "I know a secluded little vale that would serve the purpose very well."

She squeezed against him and let him lead her to the cemetery annex. Along the way, she pressed her breast against his side.

"Nefertiti?" she asked.

"Do not worry. When she misses us and sees Atli standing sentinel twenty meters behind her, she'll know. She'll probably even know where we are."

Atli ordered a new hut built for Om.

Twenty-Two

Nefertiti sent out four messengers. The first went to intercept two Viking ships off Marbella. The second went to Carthage. The third and fourth went to the Nile.

She sought passage to England from the Vikings, specifically to visit the tin mines in Cardiff. Phoenicia had red-hot commercial traffic in tin, because it could be combined with copper to make bronze. The main point, though, was that she had acquired a taste for travel and adventure. When the request was denied, she referred to Moe, who told her that although the Vikings didn't have a princess, they considered her one, but nevertheless, they refused to take her onto the Atlantic Sea. They wouldn't risk her life there, because they considered her the only meaningful princess on Earth.

That was the day she fully emerged from childhood.

Her second request of the Vikings was granted. She asked them to stand off the coast on the day she visited the Pharaoh.

The message to Carthage was to request the famous medicine woman to accompany her to the Nile to meet with the world-renowned medical conference in perpetual session and attend her as a lady in waiting with the Pharaoh. This request, too, was denied. The old woman was in no condition for a sea voyage, not even a short one. She suggested her young apprentice be given the honor and promised she would be ready to attend. Nefertiti accepted.

The third messenger was actually a spy who was ordered to listen. He shouldn't speak with anyone and remain undetected, then he would report to her everything he could learn about the Pharaoh and his family.

The fourth messenger was sent to request permission for Nefertiti to visit the Pharaoh the next diplomatic season. No agenda was given. It was suggested, however, that Nefertiti was an accomplished medicine woman who would appreciate the opportunity to visit with the renowned medical people who might be in residence during her visit.

The visit was approved, although the Pharaoh sent a spy. Both spies were detected, but they were allowed to operate and report.

The Pharaoh's spy was an old, trusted friend, who explained to the Pharaoh that he would be under Nefertiti's control within thirty minutes of meeting her. He also advised it would be a wonderful thing for Egypt, since his son, Akhenaton, was useless, while Nefertiti was not.

Nefertiti's spy reported that the Pharaoh was possibly the finest monarch in all history, but he had no creditable daughter and wanted one very much.

The Pharaoh's petition room wasn't large within the enormous edifice. People didn't reach that room until they'd gone through a sieve of public servants. The Pharaoh saw an erect figure in white gleaming in the soft morning sunlight. Nefertiti saw a man on a throne that wasn't very elevated, and she approved.

Om stepped aside to the left, because armed warriors weren't allowed within the chamber. Nefertiti entered with her two ladies in waiting. The young Carthaginian was to her left, while To-To was to her right. Prior to entering To-To moved her skirt aside a bit to reveal the blade hidden in the pleats to the guards. That was protocol and totally proper. A woman of Nefertiti's rank was entitled to be killed by her own servant rather than mauled by soldiers.

Actually, it wasn't a dagger but a throwing knife, and she had two others just in case. The young soldier saw only To-To's thigh.

The security precautions weren't needed. Within the hour, Nefertiti shared the throne with the monarch and poured him some of his best red wine.

She excused herself to meet with the College of Surgeons. As she left, the Pharaoh wondered if she would become the daughter he always wanted or his chief wife. To his great credit, he chose Egypt and let her become a daughter.

Later that evening, Nefertiti and Akhenaton, the Pharaoh's son, sat measuring each other. He saw the most-beautiful woman he ever met, a view that would be shared by men for fifty centuries. She saw a puppy, although he would be useful enough. She loved Amun and was more than fond of Petro, which was growing swiftly of its own volition.

Akhenaton and Nefertiti discussed the knotty problem of how to get her home safely and back again the following spring with the Romans knowing the route she had to take and the approximate time of her travels. He suggested that no hazardous travel was necessary. She could remain in the palace with her handmaidens in attendance and as many additional servants as she required. If she became pregnant, she would have endless competent assistance.

Nefertiti summoned Moe. They were hull down just over the western horizon before morning.

Twenty-Three

Moe explained he could outrun any Roman on any course, but that didn't matter. They only needed to know his destination and wait for him. He devised a plan and explained her part in the deception. It would be only the first of many such deceptions, all of which had to succeed.

Moe, sailing past his destination, continued west, lingering over the horizon until he saw a freighter carrying their flag. It was on its way from the tin mines in the westernmost extremity of the British Isles, Cardiff, to customers in the Mediterranean Sea.

Moe put her aboard the freighter despite her protests. She wanted to be taken on to where she could look out to the end of the world. Taking her to Cardiff would mean sailing beyond the Pillars of Hercules into a sea that Moe's ship wasn't made to handle. She was fourteen, only one year before she could have imperiously demanded such a joy ride, but not then.

Nefertiti was safely aboard the freighter while Moe sailed west to draw attention from her.

She entered the busiest time of her life. In a few months, she would turn fifteen and would become queen, married to the next Pharaoh. Akhenaton would become Amenhotep IV.

Nefertiti summoned Amun. On their way through the graveyard, she left an extra-large jug of beer with Morg. Once in the vale, she told Om that she was fifteen years old that day. She wanted him to protect her beyond the vale toward the southwest. He gave her a formal salute and with it came his admiration and love.

When Amun left her safely at her new hut, he gave her a gift to be opened later. She found a shard of sandstone like those chiseled by artisans making great works of art, with a poem from Amun on it.

I love you.
I am sure of it.
You are in my heart permanently.
You dream of standing on a cliff,
Looking west to the future.
I dream of standing beside you.
The Gods will grant us this in the next life,
Or I will come and find you,
My Queen for the ages.

Nefertiti had never heard words of love and wasn't able to take them as words of farewell. She sent for Amun, and together, they ached through the night.

Twenty-Four

The following spring, Nefertiti boarded a freighter bound for the Nile wearing a hooded gray foul-weather cape. Moe left a day earlier carrying a mannequin wearing one of her bright white gowns. The passage was uneventful except that one of the passengers, a young soldier, approached her from behind with undefined amorous intent.

Nefertiti, aware of him, hid a thole pin under her cloak. Om stood ready by the gunwale a few feet away. The approaching young man was unaware of either the thole pin or the man by the rail. He was also unaware that the lady by the mast was To-To, who casually cleared her skirt aside. His greatest sin, though, was that he didn't realize the woman he approached was actually his princess and future queen.

The thole pin came out of nowhere and struck his bronze helmet with surprising force. The boy heard a sound like every bronze bell in Egypt being struck simultaneously. When the boatswain demanded his name, he couldn't think of an answer.

"Take him to the captain," Nefertiti ordered. "Tell him this business is in his jurisdiction. He should also consider the possibility of sparing his life. He hasn't touched me, and as a soldier, he should be punished only for failing to reach his objective."

The bosun laughed and bowed deeply. When he straightened, he was still grinning. Those in the crew immediately passed the story along.

They tied up at a commercial dock and awaited the royal barge. By the time it reached the palace, the Pharaoh had left his throne and stood at the top of the stone steps, smiling down at Nefertiti. He heard her quote and liked it.

He welcomed her as Nefertiti, princess and future queen of the Egyptians.

EPILOGUE

Nefertiti was orphaned before her fifth birthday. History took no further note of her until she was fifteen. This fictional account attempts to describe those missing ten years.

Nefertiti married Amenhotep IV and joined him on the throne as Pharaoh. She ruled for twelve years, bore six daughters, and was deceased at age forty, still a beauty.

Amenhotep III was almost certainly the wisest of all the Pharaohs of ancient Egypt. Some were more colorful, such as Ramses, but none faced the challenges of the mid-fourteenth century B.C. as competently as he. By that time, men had left the trees and then the caves. They were finished with the Stone and Copper Ages and were well into the Bronze Age. The population was growing, as was commerce and peace. Society was basically socialist in nature, having evolved from a loose amalgamation of tribes.

Commercial convoys traveled without significant armaments, because everyone wanted the cargos to get through. Those ships hauled the riches of the East and the West. Crops raised in one part of the known world began to be enjoyed in another. Egypt and Greece saw advances in medical knowledge that benefited all.

Yet someone with Amenhotep III's intelligence would have seen the storm clouds gathering for the future. With the growth of prosperity never seen before, creating larger populations and greater sea power, new priorities would emerge. Some men would invade other countries to take the people's possessions, gain martial fame, satisfy an ego, or answer the prodding of paranoia.

Amenhotep III thought he could protect his people from future harm. Prosperity was a good thing, and he didn't want to interfere with its growth. Population increase came without his help, and that would continue, as peripheral peoples were absorbed with their free consent almost daily. Sea power was in his hands, because all the sailors of all countries were of one mind and would support each other almost without asking.

The weakness for Egypt was his son and heir. He created two solutions for that. He could have him assassinated or get him a strong queen. He couldn't kill his own son, but he had a good queen waiting. Perhaps he should have unleashed Nefertiti's fullest potential by sending his son on a lifetime safari in Timbuktu.

His wedding gift to Nefertiti was a brace of Egyptian hounds. That breed didn't survive to the present day, but they resembled Rhodesian Ridgebacks. They had high intelligence, great speed, webbed feet, monstrous ugly jaws, and the ability to run in the desert for two days without water. They had been raised in southern Africa and were brought to Egypt by the Phoenicians. Nefertiti could not have been more pleased.

However, her husband had a fatal flaw. He had the unerring ability to snatch defeat from the jaws of victory. He announced that Egypt should become monotheistic, not polytheistic. That hurt all Egyptians badly. They'd been polytheistic for as long as anyone could remember. They didn't disrespect Aten, the new sun god, but he didn't always heed their pleas. The goddess of the hearth and a host of lesser deities were always a comfort.

Then he named Nefertiti, an admirer of no god, as High Priestess of the Sun God. Artisans stopped work and left their chisels on the sites they recently excavated. Egypt dissolved from within during the following centuries.

Alexander the Great came and named a city after himself. Then the Romans came and made a trollop of a later, lesser Egyptian queen, forgetting that when they came, the Egyptians were behind them.

Adolf Hitler searched history to find the ancestry of the modern Germans and found it in Nefertiti's husband. He found a soul brother across the centuries. In Hitler's mind, they were one megalomaniac, but there was nothing tangible left of Akhenaton to recover, so he took Nefertiti's bust as a surrogate.

Egypt was an ancient superpower. When visitors came, they were too few in number to be effective. Egypt absorbed them until they adopted mummification for themselves.

Over all the passing centuries, though, Nefertiti lived on. She was known by all in that small world as the most-majestic and regal of all queens. Her bust was accurately carved by an old friend, Thutmose of Amarna, as she stood for him in his shop in 1340 BC.

That same bust can be seen in the Neues Museum in Berlin, Germany.

Nefertiti is Charles W Fowler's debut novel.